January 2023

To Hero

Have fun with the story!

Ila Maryanova

To Maya, Milo, and Max.

And to the world's best supporters~
my mom and my husband.

"And whatever you do, whether in word or deed,
do it all in the name of the Lord Jesus, giving thanks
to God the Father through him." (Colossians 3:17)

L.M.

 ISBN 978-1-952954-80-1

Published by Storybook Genius, LLC.

On a burning hot day in the savanna in Africa...

Am I a black zebra with white stripes
OR a white zebra with black stripes?

Maybe Butterfly knows?

Hi, Butterfly! Am I a black zebra with white stripes OR a white zebra with black stripes?

What would you rather be?
I want to be me. Only, I don't know who that is.

I think I see a white zebra with black stripes on this side, but I see a black zebra with white stripes on the other side. Are you OK with that?

Never mind. That doesn't answer my question. I'll ask Owl.

Owl, am I a black zebra with white stripes OR a white zebra with black stripes?

I don't know. That's a great question. Now...where is my book about animals?

Thank you, but I can't...

Let me read about zebras and get back to you.

Never mind. I need an answer now. I'll ask Turtle.

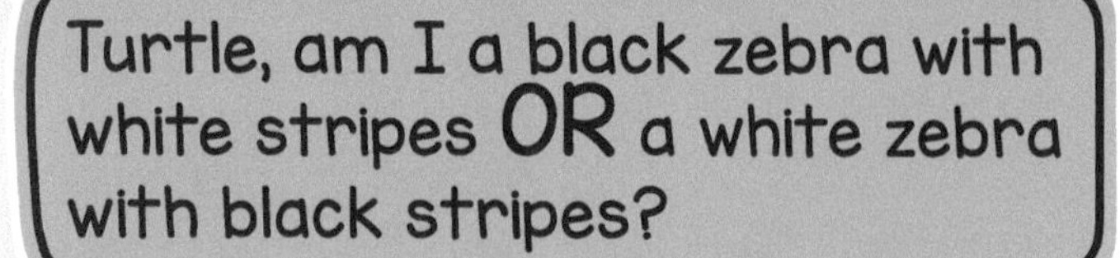

Let me help you find that out! I can't see very well, but my friend Ant might know...or my friend Snail might know...or, wait, Worm might know. Let's go!

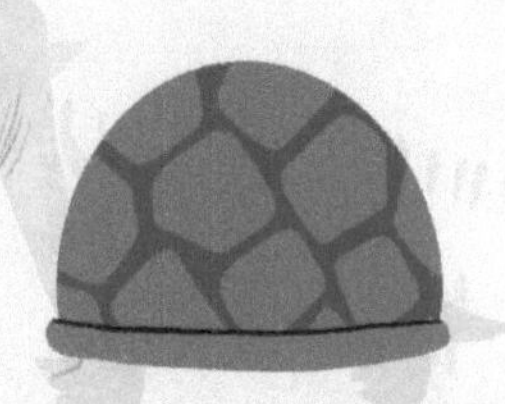

Come on, quick, let's go find out!

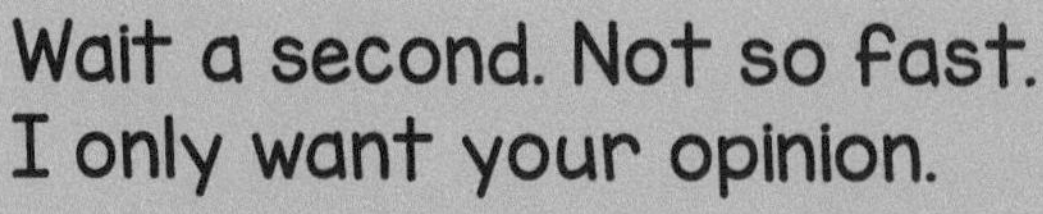

Never mind. I need an answer now. I'll ask Giraffe.

Giraffe, am I a black zebra with white stripes OR a white zebra with black stripes?
Do I look like an information desk?
Are you OK? Why are you so rude? I just asked a question. That's all.

I don't even know who I am. Am I a brown giraffe with a tan pattern or a tan giraffe with brown spots? You are not the only one with problems!
Never mind. I'll ask Mouse.

Mouse, am I a black zebra with white stripes OR a white zebra with black stripes?
Why are you asking me? Is this a trick question?
I just want your opinion.

Never mind. I'll ask Elephant.

This has to be a trick. No one asks for my opinion. Goodbye.

Elephant, am I a black zebra with white stripes OR a white zebra with black stripes?
That is a great question! I like it. Have you been to the new jump park?
No, I haven't. What do you think I am?

Want to come? It will be so much fun!
That doesn't answer my question. I'll ask Lion.

Lion, am I a black zebra with white stripes OR a white zebra with black stripes?

You are in my territory! Get out of here before I eat you.
No need to be so angry. Do you think I am a black...

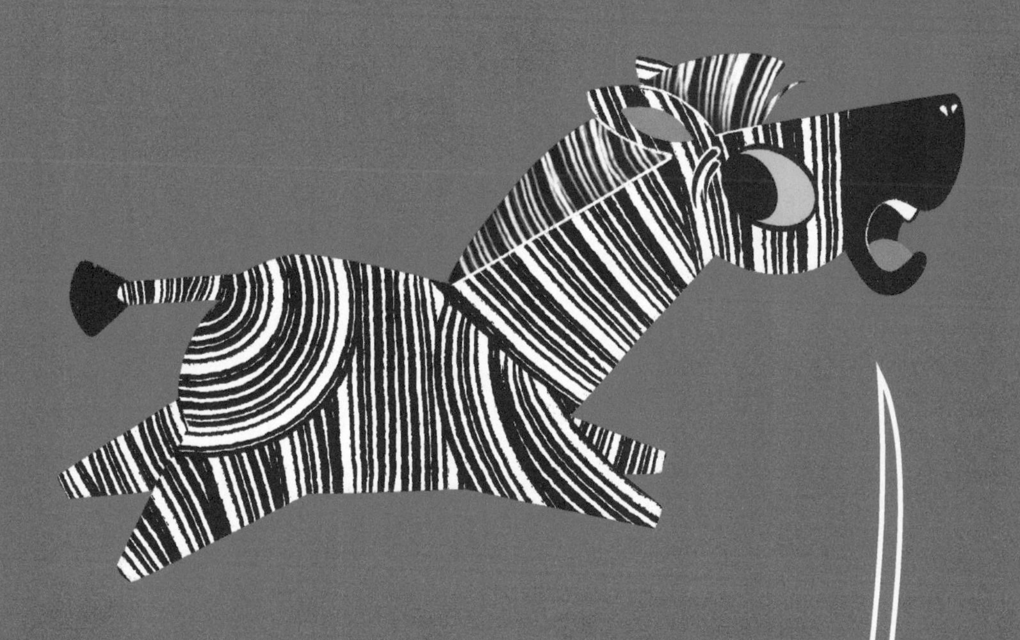

I don't care what you are. I wouldn't care if your black and white stripes were yellow or pink or blue! You would still be a yummy ZEBRA with yummy meat on your bones. If you don't get out of here, you'll be my next meal.

Never mind. I'll ask Chameleon.

Whew, that was close. Nice to see you, Chameleon. Am I a black zebra with white stripes or a white zebra with black stripes?
Zebra, you are beautiful! I love the clear distinction between white and black.

You turned white and black, too. How did you do that? What is your actual color?

It's just who I am.
Let me count how many white
and how many black stripes
you have. That might get
us the answer.

Never mind.
That won't answer
my question.

Am I a black zebra with white stripes OR a white zebra with black stripes?
What if I'll never know the answer? No one could really help me.
...Ooooooh. Hold on. I think I'm getting it!
Lion...oh, he was so scary! But he said...

I am a ZEBRA

with black AND white stripes!

CPSIA information can be obtained
at www.ICGtesting.com
Printed in the USA
BVHW091500111222
653958BV00003B/45

* 9 7 8 1 9 5 2 9 5 4 8 0 1 *

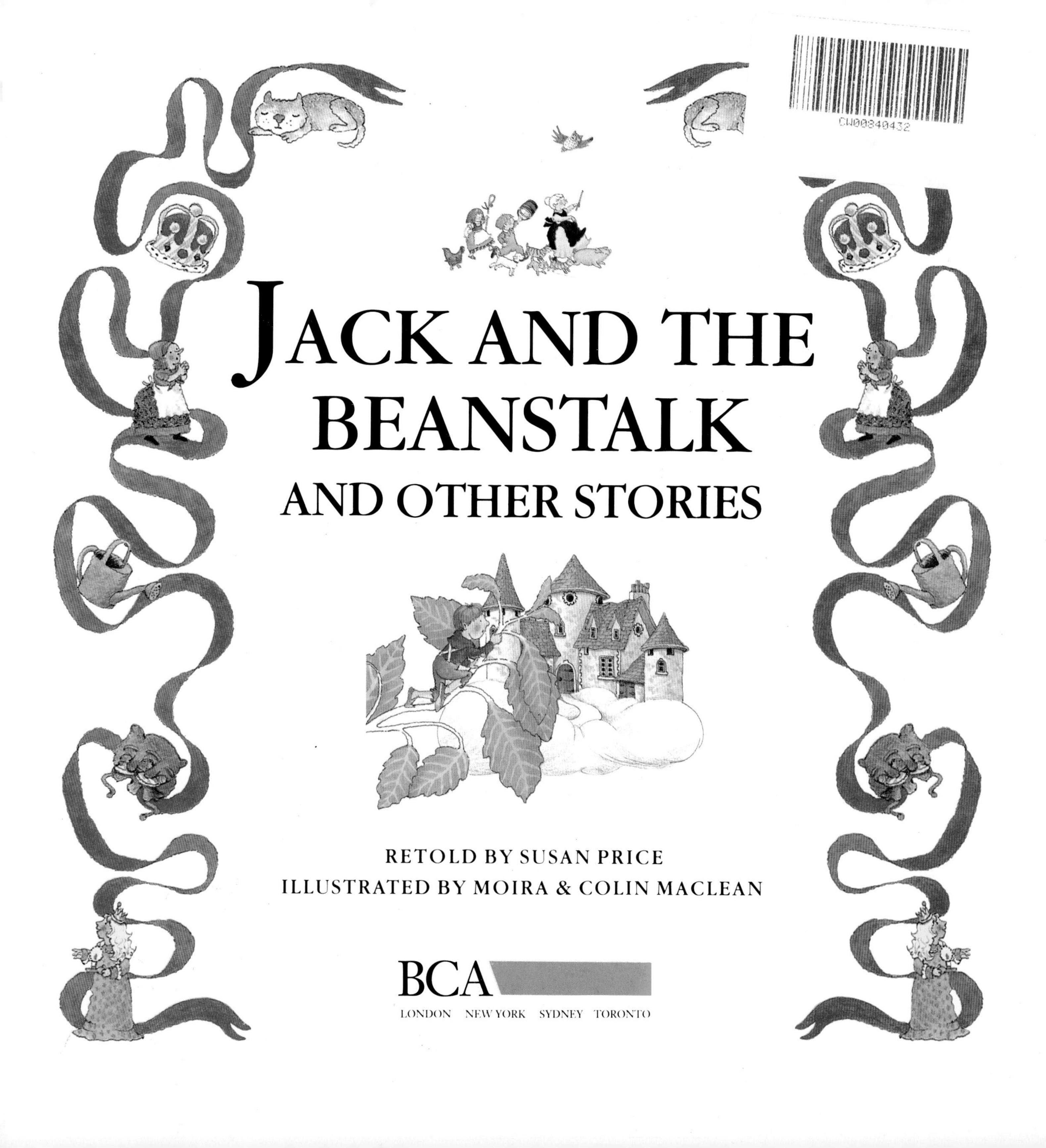

JACK AND THE BEANSTALK AND OTHER STORIES

RETOLD BY SUSAN PRICE

ILLUSTRATED BY MOIRA & COLIN MACLEAN

BCA

LONDON NEW YORK SYDNEY TORONTO

This edition published 1992 by BCA by arrangement with
Kingfisher Books, Grisewood & Dempsey Ltd,
Elsley House, 24–30 Great Titchfield Street, London W1P 7AD

The material in this edition was previously published by Kingfisher Books in
The Kingfisher Treasury of Nursery Stories (1990).

CN 1903

Printed and bound in Spain

CONTENTS

JACK AND THE BEANSTALK

Once upon a time there was a poor widow who had one son, and his name was Jack. Jack was no help to his mother, because he was lazy and only wanted to lie in front of the fire all day. "You never do anything," she always said to him. "And when you do, you never do it right!"

They had no money at all, and the only thing they had was their old cow. One day Jack's mother said, "Jack, take the old cow to market and sell her for the highest price you can get."

It was a long walk to market, and Jack didn't want to go, but he had no choice. He tied a rope around the old cow's neck and set off, as slowly as he could.

He hadn't gone very far when he met a man. "That's a stringy old thing of a cow," the man said. "Where are you taking her?"

"To market, to sell her," said Jack.

"You won't get much for that old thing," said the man.

"How much are you asking for her?"

"How much are you offering?" asked Jack.

The man put his hand in his pocket and pulled something out. "Five beans – and you won't get any more for that old creature at market!"

"That may be," said Jack, "but my mother will be furious if I go home with nothing but five beans. Even five pennies would be better."

"But these are magic beans," said the man. "They will make your fortune."

"Done!" said Jack, because he really couldn't be bothered to walk all the way to market. So the man gave

him the five beans and Jack gave the man the cow, and then went home.

"Back already?" said his mother. "What did you get for the cow?"

Jack took the beans from his pocket and showed them to his mother. "Beans!" she said. "Five beans! Why, you useless great lump!" She threw the beans out of the

window. Then she sent Jack to bed. He didn't even get a chance to explain that the beans were magic and would make their fortune.

When Jack woke up the next morning, the house was dark, as if it were still night. Something was blocking the window.

Jack ran outside and saw a huge beanstalk that grew up and up until it disappeared into the clouds. "They *were* magic beans," Jack said to himself. "I wonder what's up there." He started to climb the beanstalk, to find out what was at the top.

Jack climbed up and up and up, all the way to the top. There he found a path, leading through the clouds to a great big castle.

Jack knocked on the door. A huge woman opened it. She looked surprised to see him. "What are you doing here?" she asked. "Don't you know that a giant lives here, a giant who eats boys?"

Jack said, "But I've climbed so high and walked so far. I'm hungry – thirsty too."

"Come in," said the woman, "But you mustn't stay long."

Inside the castle, Jack and the woman got talking. All too soon, noisy footsteps were coming up the path.

"It's my husband, the giant!" said the woman. "Quick! Hide!"

Jack jumped into an empty pot by the stove and pulled down the lid.

The door opened and in came the giant. He sniffed the air and said,

"Fee, fi, fo, fum,
I smell the blood of an Englishman.
Be he alive or be he dead,
I'll grind his bones to make my bread!"

"How you go on," said the giant's wife. "There's no one here. Now sit down and eat your dinner."

So the giant sat down and ate his dinner. Then he took out a grubby-looking purse, opened it and tipped it upside-down. Out fell a great heap of gold. The giant closed the purse, opened it again – and it was filled with gold once more!

Jack was peeping out of his pot and saw. "If my mother and I had that purse," he thought, "we'd never be poor again." He made up his mind that he was going to take that purse home with him, come what may.

He watched and waited until the giant went over to his chair in front of the fire, kicked off his boots and went to sleep. Then Jack crept out of the pot, grabbed the purse – and ran for his life!

Out of the castle he ran, along the path, down the beanstalk and into his house, shouting, "Mother! Mother! Look!"

Jack's mother was amazed that her lazy son had been so brave. She looked at the purse and said, "We shall never be poor again. Promise me that you won't climb the beanstalk any more. It's dangerous."

Jack promised he wouldn't.

With the money that the purse gave them, they were much happier than before, but Jack couldn't forget the castle. One day, while his mother was out, he climbed the beanstalk again.

When Jack knocked on the castle door, the giant's wife opened it and said, "You again! If the giant finds you here – well, he'll eat you raw!"

"Oh, I'll be long gone before he gets back," Jack said. "But I must have a sit-down and something to eat and drink. I've come such a long way."

The kind woman took him in. Jack wanted to stay until the giant came home, so he got her talking until she forgot all about the time passing.

Then they heard the giant coming home.

Jack opened the cupboard under the sink and crawled inside. In came the giant, sniffing the air.

"Fee, fi, fo, fum,
I smell the blood of an Englishman.
Be he alive or be he dead,
I'll have his blood to sauce my bread!"

"Oh, don't go on," said the giant's wife. "There's no one here. Eat your food, you big lump."

So the giant sat down to his dinner. When he'd finished, he brought out a beautiful red hen. He stroked her feathers gently and the hen laid eggs for him. Not ordinary eggs, but eggs of beautiful shining gold!

Jack waited until the giant had fallen asleep by the fire. Then he crept out of the cupboard, grabbed the hen – and ran for his life!

Out of the castle, along the path, down the beanstalk and into his house he ran, shouting, "Mother! Look!"

When Jack's mother saw the hen and the eggs, she could hardly believe her eyes. She made him promise, *promise,* never to climb the beanstalk again.

Jack promised.

With all the gold from the purse, and the golden eggs from the hen, they were rich. But Jack couldn't forget the castle. He climbed the beanstalk again.

When the giant's wife opened the door and saw who it was, she said, "Go away! I dare not let you in." But she was a kind woman, and Jack persuaded her to let him in after all. They got talking, and the giant's wife soon forgot all about the time – until she heard her husband coming home.

Jack crawled under the washtub and hid. In came the giant, sniffing the air.

"Fee, fi, fo, fum,
I smell the blood of an
Englishman . . ."

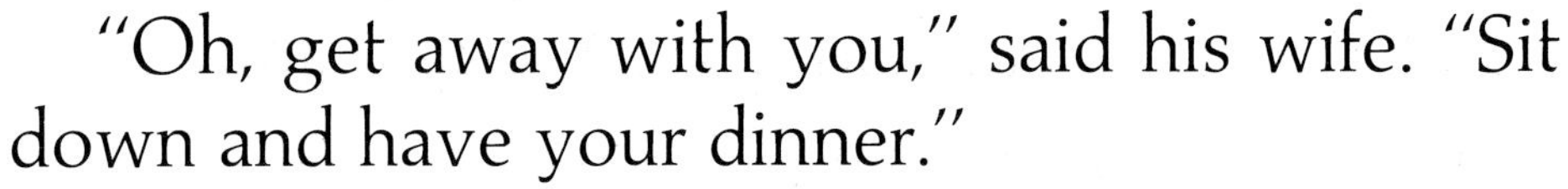

"Oh, get away with you," said his wife. "Sit down and have your dinner."

When the giant had eaten his dinner, he fetched a beautiful golden harp. "Play, harp," he said, and the harp played beautiful music, all by itself!

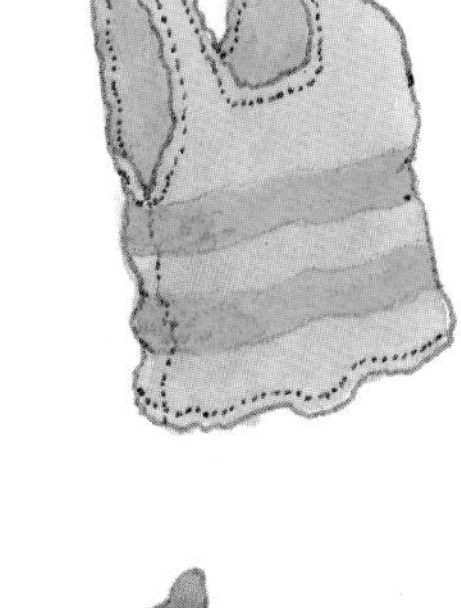

Jack waited until the giant fell asleep, crept out, grabbed the harp – and ran for his life!

But as he ran, the harp cried out, "Master! Master!" The giant woke up, jumped to his feet and ran after Jack with great big strides.

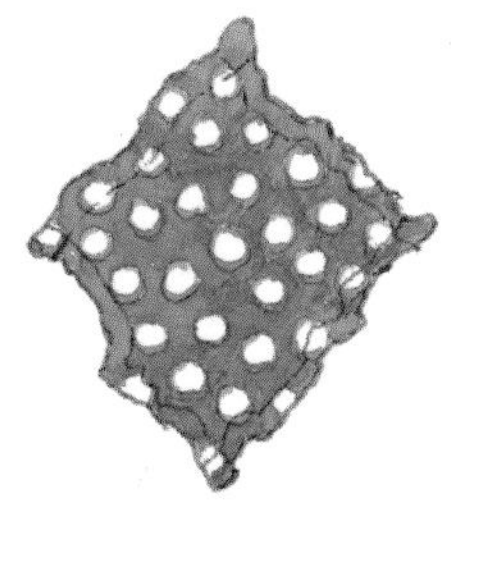

Jack reached the beanstalk first, and started climbing down as fast as he could. But the giant reached the beanstalk too, and began climbing down after Jack.

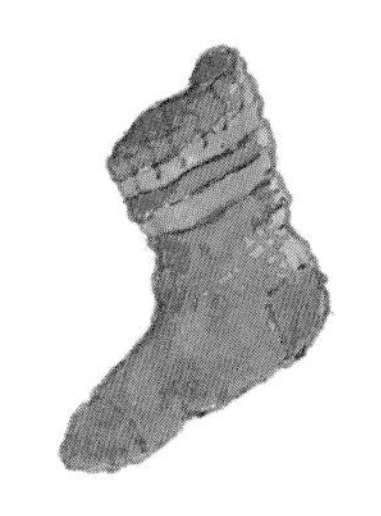

Jack reached the ground first, dropped the harp and snatched up an axe his mother used to chop wood. He began to chop down the beanstalk.

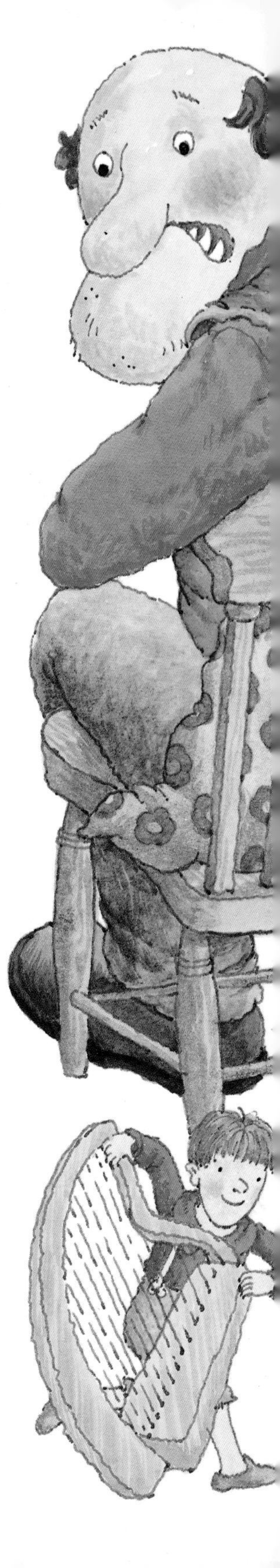

He chopped and chopped and chopped, and at last he chopped right through. Down came the beanstalk, and down came the giant. With a CRASH! the giant landed on his head, and that was the end of him.

So Jack and his mother had the purse of gold, and the hen that laid golden eggs, and the harp that played all by itself, and they lived happily in comfort all the rest of their lives.

And that is the end of the story.

THE PRINCESS AND THE PEA

Once upon a time there was a Prince, and he wanted to marry a Princess; but she had to be a *real* Princess. He travelled all over the world in his search for a Princess, and Princesses he found in plenty; but whether they were *real* Princesses he couldn't decide, for now one thing, now another, seemed not quite right. At last he returned home to his palace and was very sad, because he wished so much to have a real Princess for his wife.

One evening there was a fearful storm; thunder crashed, lightning flashed, rain poured down from the sky in torrents – and it was dark as dark can be. All at once there was heard a knocking at the door. The Prince's father, the old King himself, went out to open it.

A Princess stood outside; but gracious! what a sight she was, out there in the rain. Water trickled down from her hair; water dripped from her clothes; water ran in at the toes of her shoes and out at the heels. And yet she said she was a real Princess.

"We shall soon see about that!" thought the old Queen, but she didn't say anything.

She went into the bedroom, took all the clothes off the bed and laid one dried pea on the mattress. Then she piled twenty more mattresses on top of it, and twenty

eiderdowns over that. On this the girl who said she was a real Princess was to lie all night.

The next morning she was asked how she had slept.

"Oh, shockingly!" she replied. "I haven't even closed my eyes. I don't know what was in my bed, but there was something hard that has bruised me all over."

They saw at once that she must be a *real* Princess, for she had felt the little dried pea through twenty eider-downs and twenty mattresses. Only a *real* Princess could have such delicate skin.

So the Prince asked the Princess to marry him, and the pea was put in a museum, as a curiosity. You may go yourself and see it.

Now, wasn't that a *real* story?

THE LITTLE RED HEN

Once upon a time, in a farmyard, there lived a busy little red hen and her chicks.

A dog, a cat and a pig lived there too, but they were lazy. The dog and the cat slept nearly all day, and the pig was always either eating or lying in his mud patch.

One day, the little red hen found a grain of wheat. "Who will help me plant this grain?" she asked.

"Not I," said the dog.

"Not I," said the cat.

"Not I," said the pig. They were all too idle.

"Then I shall do it, and my chicks will help me," said the little red hen. She scratched a hole in the earth and planted the grain of wheat, and her chicks helped her.

But the earth was dry and the wheat couldn't grow.

"Who will help me water the wheat?" asked the little red hen.

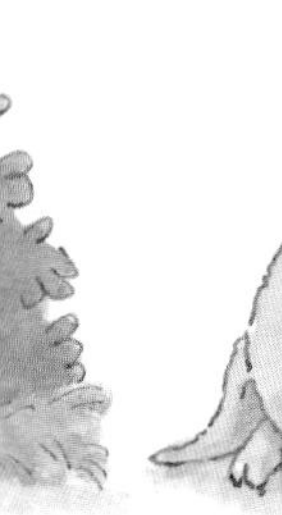

"Not I," said the dog.
"Not I," said the cat.
"Not I," said the pig.
"Then I shall do it, and my chicks will help me," said the little red hen. She carried water from the pump and watered the wheat, and her chicks helped her.

After that, the wheat grew and grew until it was ready to be harvested. "Who will help me harvest the wheat?" asked the little red hen.

"Not I," said the dog.
"Not I," said the cat.
"Not I," said the pig.
"Then I shall do it, and my chicks will help me." And she and her chicks cut down the wheat.

To separate the good grain from the husk, the wheat

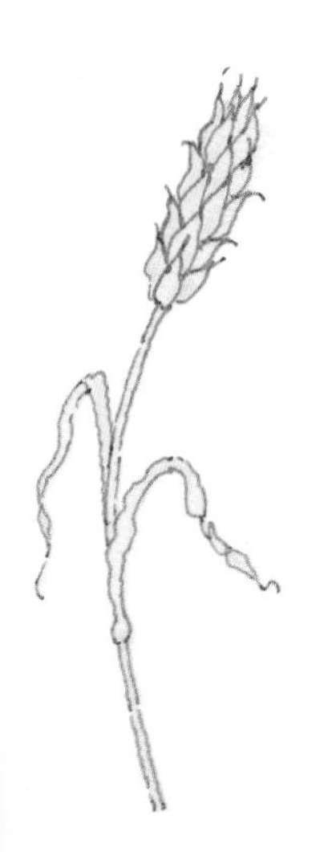

had to be threshed and winnowed. "Who will help me thresh the wheat?" asked the little red hen.

"Not I," said the dog.

"Not I," said the cat.

"Not I," said the pig.

"Then I shall do it," said the little red hen, "and my chicks will help me." She and her chicks worked hard threshing the wheat and throwing it into the air for the husks to blow away.

"Who will help me carry the grain to the mill, to have it ground into flour?" asked the little red hen.

"Not I," said the dog.

"Not I," said the cat.

"Not I," said the pig.

"Then I shall do it, and my chicks will help me." The little red hen and her chicks carried the grain all the way to the mill. When it was ground, they carried the flour all the way home.

"Now, who will help me bake a cake?" asked the little red hen.

"Not I," said the dog.

"Not I," said the cat.

"Not I," said the pig.

"Then I'll bake it myself," said the little red hen, "and my chicks will help me." She set to work and baked a cake, and her chicks helped her. When the cake was ready, the little red hen took it out of the oven. A beautiful, sweet, spicy, warm smell drifted over the farmyard. The dog lifted his head and sniffed. The cat twitched her nose and sniffed. The pig sat up in his mud patch and sniffed.

"Who will help me eat this cake?" asked the little red hen.

"I will!" said the dog.

"And I will!" said the cat.

"Me too!" said the pig.

"Oh no you won't!" said the little red hen. "Not a slice, not a crumb. My chicks and I did all the work, so my chicks and I shall eat all the cake!"

They did, and a fine cake it was. Now all the cake is finished, and so is this story.